Cheeky Mouse and Cool Cat live in Happy
Tail Town, not far from Happy Tail Wood.
They are the best of friends and you can
read about their adventures in the books
in this series.

British Library Cataloguing in Publication Data
Gatehouse, John
    The ghost of Happy Tail Wood. —
    (Cheeky Mouse and Cool Cat; no. 2)
    I. Title   II. Leographics   III. Series
    823'.914[J]   PZ7
    ISBN 0-7214-1011-1

First edition
Published by Ladybird Books Ltd Loughborough Leicestershire UK
Ladybird Books Inc Lewiston Maine 04240 USA
© MCMLXXXVI by BLUEBIRD TOYS PLC
*Cheeky Mouse and Cool Cat are trademarks of Bluebird Toys PLC and are used with
permission.*
© LADYBIRD BOOKS LTD MCMLXXXVII
Printed in England

The ghost of Happy Tail Wood

written by JOHN GATEHOUSE
illustrations by LEOGRAPHICS

Ladybird Books

Cheeky Mouse was sitting in the armchair at Hide-E-Hole house reading a book of ghost stories.

"Gorgonzola! This is exciting!" he gasped, his whiskers standing on end!

Cool Cat laughed. "What rubbish," he chuckled. "There are no such things as ghosts."

Cool Cat went back into the kitchen and decided to play a funny trick on his friend. He took down a tin of flour from the cupboard and pulled off the lid. Then he shook the flour all over himself and soon he was as white as a...*ghost!*

Cheeky was tucking into a delicious bowl of cheese porridge when Cool Cat crept back into the room.

Cool Cat tried hard not to giggle as he wailed in a ghostly voice, *"Whoooo-oooh! I am the ghost of Hide-E-Hole house and I have come to haaaauuuunnnnt you!"*

Poor Cheeky! He was so surprised to see the ghostly white figure that he let out a loud cry.

"Eeek!" he screamed, leaping out of his chair.

Up into the air went the porridge pot. It did a little somersault...and landed on Cool Cat's head!

The porridge ran down Cool Cat's nose and plip-plopped onto his feet.

"It's all sticky!" he groaned.

Cheeky laughed when he saw that the "ghost" was really his friend. "You don't look very ghostly now, Cool Cat!" he said.

"I'm going for a bath," muttered Cool Cat, feeling very grumpy.

Cheeky chuckled as Cool Cat left the room with the porridge plip-plopping behind him.

Then Cheeky had an idea. He went to the fancy dress cupboard. He took out a scary monster mask. "I'll put this on and scare Cool Cat when he comes back," he grinned.

*   *   *

A little time later a sparkling-clean-and-smelling-like-primroses Cool Cat came back from his bath.

"Boo!" shouted Cheeky very loudly. And he jumped out at Cool Cat from behind the door.

Cool Cat looked once...he looked twice... and then he burst out laughing.

"Ha! Ha! Ha! You *do* look silly in that mask, Cheeky!" he chuckled.

"You're not meant to laugh," said Cheeky, crossly. "You're meant to be scared."

"Nothing scares *me*," Cool Cat boasted.
"I'm as brave as brave can be!"

Cheeky took off the mask. "It's time for us
to go to Happy Tail Wood to pick
blackberries for tomorrow's breakfast," he
said quickly, not wanting to hear stories of
how brave Cool Cat was.

But Cool Cat was still boasting as they came to the wood. ''Oh, yes! Nothing frightens me! Why, if I saw a ghost I'd pull a funny face and scare *him* away instead!''

''You take this trail,'' Cheeky said, pointing ahead. ''And I'll take this one.'' And they both set off, each carrying a basket for the blackberries.

Cool Cat skipped happily down the path,
singing to himself. The path was quite
narrow and was lined with tall green trees.
It became darker and darker as Cool Cat
went deeper and deeper into the wood.
Soon it was very dark indeed.

"Ooooh! It is a *little* s-scary," Cool Cat
whispered. Then he puffed out his chest
bravely. "N-Not that I'm scared, of course."
He began to whistle to cheer himself up.

Then he heard a low wailing sound which
seemed to be coming closer and closer.
"WOO-AH! WOO-AH!"

"I-Is t-that y-you, C-Cheeky?" Cool Cat whispered.

And suddenly a white-sheeted figure appeared before him!

"Oh, Cheeky!" laughed Cool Cat. "Fancy dressing up in a white sheet to try and scare me! You look nothing like a ghost!"

"Hello, Cool Cat," said Cheeky, coming up behind him. "Who are you talking to?"

"Oh, hello, Cheeky," said Cool Cat, still chuckling. "I'm talking to you, all dressed up in that white sheet, pretending to be a g-g-ghost!"

Cool Cat looked at Cheeky and then at the white-sheeted figure.

"Waaah! A ghostie!" Cool Cat screamed at the top of his voice and leapt into a bush to hide!

Cheeky (who was feeling rather nervous himself) was surprised to see that the ghost was crying.

"BOO HOO!" sobbed the ghost sadly. "No one likes me! They all scream and run away when they see me coming!"

Cool Cat poked his head out from inside the bush. He felt very sorry for the ghost who seemed so sad.

"Don't cry," said Cool Cat kindly. "I wasn't *really* scared of you."

"Yes, don't cry," said Cheeky. "We'll be your friends, if you like."

"Will you really?" asked the ghost, cheering up a little. Then he looked sad again.

"But that won't stop everyone else running away when they see me," he sighed.

Cheeky Mouse thought for a moment. "How do you say 'hello' when you meet someone?" he asked.

"Like this," said the ghost. And he jumped up at Cool Cat and Cheeky Mouse, shouting, *"WOO-OOO-AHAH!"*

Cool Cat screamed and jumped back into the bush.

"That's it!" laughed Cheeky. "People wouldn't be so frightened of you if you didn't go around wailing and jumping out at them!"

"Oh!" said the ghost with a happy smile. "I hadn't thought of that! Well, from now on I shall be extra nice when I meet someone."

Then the ghost took his new friends to the best blackberry bush in Happy Tail Wood.

When they had filled their baskets to the top, Cool Cat and Cheeky Mouse said goodbye to the ghost and made their way back home.

"Of course, *I* wasn't scared of the ghost," boasted Cool Cat as they walked along the path. "I told you, I'm not frightened of anything!"

They had almost reached Hide-E-Hole house
when Cool Cat stopped still. There, in the
garden, he saw three white-sheeted figures
flying up and down!

"G-G-Ghosties!" he cried. And dropping his basket of blackberries he ran off down the path!

Cheeky Mouse laughed and laughed when he saw what was really in the garden. "Ha! Ha! Silly Cool Cat! They're not ghosts! It's the washing blowing in the wind! Ha! Ha! Ha!"